EDINBURGH CITY LIBRARIES

Please return/renew this item by the last date shown.
To renew quote your borrower number.
www.edinburgh.gov.uk/libraries

Portobello Library
14 Rosefield Avenue
Edinburgh
EH15 1AU
0131 529 5558

08 DEC 2015

Race Ahead

with Reading

The Egyptian Cat Mystery

By Penny Dolan

Illustrated by Andy Elkerton

W

FRANKLIN WATTS

LONDON • SYDNEY

Chapter 1
The Egyptian Cat

"Hurry up!" cried Jed, running up the steps and into the museum. He and his big sister Ruby sped to their favourite spot: the Egyptian Galleries. They liked to look at all the precious treasures and statues and gaze at the mummies in their decorated cases.

Today the galleries were almost empty.

Jed and Ruby could look at the ancient

wall-paintings for ages.

"I'd like to be an Egyptian Princess and sail

along the River Nile," said Ruby, dreamily.

"Well, I'd like to ride in a chariot," Jed told

her, "and feel the horses going really fast."

Then they spotted a poster:

"HAVE FUN ON A MUSEUM SLEEPOVER!"

"I'd like to do that," Jed sighed.

"Me too," said Ruby, but they both knew

it would cost too much.

After a while, Jed's tummy rumbled.

Ruby's did too.

"Snack time," Ruby giggled.

"I'm starving."

They sat down on a bench. Ruby opened up
her backpack.

"Yum, yum," she said.

"Ugh! Prawn cocktail crisps? Yuk!"
grumbled Jed.

No Eating

"She'd like them," Ruby joked, pointing
at the carved cat who sat proudly on a
pillar nearby.

"No way," Jed told Ruby. "That cat is too grand for your smelly fishy crisps."

Jed really admired the Egyptian cat.

She had a narrow gold collar round her neck and tiny golden discs hanging from her ears.

"Sitting there forever must be so boring,"
Jed said. "Maybe there's a magical day
when she comes back to life?"
Ruby laughed. Just then the sun shone
through the windows and the cat's face
glowed. Jed was sure she had smiled at him.
"Don't be silly," he told himself.

While they nibbled their apples, Ruby told
Jed a tale about the ghostly Egyptian
Princess. She was said to haunt the corridors
of the museum although nobody knew why.
Jed liked the story, even if it wasn't true.

A scowling workman wheeled a trolley along the gallery towards them. He glared hard at Ruby and Jed as if he wanted them to move.

"Shall we go?" whispered Jed.

"No," said Ruby. "We're allowed to sit here. Although maybe not eat here," she added nervously, eyeing a sign. "Oops!"

No Eating

The man unloaded a set of screens. He set them up all around the cat's statue. Then he slapped a big "Keep Out" sticker on the outside and went inside, all by himself.

"That's not fair," grumbled Jed.

"Now we can't see our cat."

KEEP
OUT

11

Chapter 2
A Strange Event

As the clock struck three, the man behind the screens started chanting. He sang in an odd, high voice.

Bong
Bong

Aaaaiiii-Ooooooo-Ahhhhhhh

"That's a weird song. What's going on?" asked Jed.

"I don't know." Ruby frowned.

"Did you see that strange amulet hanging around his neck?"

Suddenly they heard shuffling and a sharp,
cat-like cry. The man came out from the
screens holding a big cardboard box, and
then walked quickly away.

"That looked just like a pet-carrier,"
said Ruby. Jed peeked behind the screens.
The beautiful Egyptian cat had gone!

EGYPTIAN
CAT

"That man does work for the museum, doesn't he?" Jed wondered.

"He must do," said Ruby, uncertain. Just then her phone beeped. "Anyway, it's time to go home, Jed. Mum says hurry up!"

They took the back staircase, down
to the gloomy corridor and the heavy
revolving doors. Jed was about to go
through when he stopped. A shadowy figure
stared back at him through the dark glass. It
wasn't his face. It wasn't Ruby's face either.

It was a ghostly woman. She wore a wide
jewelled braid around her long straight hair.
Her dark eyes were lined with paint and she
looked sad and angry. Jed knew only Ruby
was behind him.

"It's the Egyptian Princess!" he gasped.

"Stop messing about, Jed. Just go through the doors," Ruby grumbled.

"I can see her!" Jed cried.

"No way!" Ruby pushed Jed into the revolving doors and immediately the figure disappeared. Suddenly Ruby stopped and stared. Then she gulped and pushed through the doors after Jed. Her eyes were wide. "I saw her too! What does she want?"

Their bus was at the stop, so Ruby grabbed Jed's hand and they rushed on board.

"Stay next to me," she ordered. "Look out for our stop."

The crowded bus inched through the traffic.

Suddenly Jed froze. Further along the bus sat the strange man from the museum. He wore an ordinary coat. His eyes were closed, and he was holding the pet-carrier.

"Ruby," Jed hissed. "Look! I'm sure he's got the cat!"

"We can't do anything," Ruby replied, as the bus squeezed under a railway bridge.

All at once, they saw a face appear next to them. The Egyptian Princess! She seemed to be speaking, one silent word at a time: "Free the cat," she begged.

Immediately, they glanced at the cardboard box. It was bulging a bit. Then one edge split and a black paw poked out.

"He has got a cat in there,"
Ruby whispered.

"Not any old cat," Jed told her. "It's the cat from the museum. Today's her magic day and he's cat-napped her."

It was all very well for the Princess to ask them to save the cat, but how?

Chapter 3
Cat Rescue!

Their bus stop was coming up quite soon.
Ruby and Jed went towards the door. The
man was fast asleep. Now they could see
two paws were clawing away at the gap.
Jed thought about the ghostly Princess.
"Free the cat!" That's what she'd asked.

So, carefully, Jed pushed one leg against the pet-carrier. As he pushed, the hole gaped wider. Quickly, the cat slid out and smiled up at them. As the door of the bus opened, Ruby and Jed glanced at each other.

"Go!" Ruby hissed.

They shot out and away down the nearest street, the cat at their heels. They saw the man wake and struggle to his feet but the doors had already closed. Too late! He was trapped inside the bus.

Jed and Ruby had saved the mysterious cat. "But what do we do with her now?" Ruby said.

The cat walked along between them,
proudly holding up her tail. The street-lights
shone on her golden collar and the glinting
rings in her ears.

"What shall we tell Mum?" Ruby said,
as she unlocked the front door.
"She'll be home soon."

Pets were not allowed in the flats, but that did not bother the cat. Meowing happily, she prowled around and made herself at home. She chose a corner in Jed's room, just behind the chair, and curled up into a ball. Not a moment too soon!

Mum came in, beaming.

"Did you have a good time at

the museum?"

"Listen, kids, after we've eaten, I've got to

pop out for a while. Mrs Brown from next

door will look in on you. Is that okay?"

Ruby and Jed sighed happily.

Once Mrs Brown had turned on the TV, they could go and look after the magical black cat.

"She's so beautiful," said Ruby.

The cat woke, gave a long elegant stretch and sprang up onto the windowsill. She nuzzled at Jed's books about the Egyptians.

Suddenly she paused. She stared at the round glass paperweight. Inside the glass sphere was a model of an ancient pyramid. All at once, the cat's eyes became two green full moons.

"Meow!" she cried, calling the children closer to her.

Chapter 4
Another World

Ruby and Jed felt the glass globe growing larger and larger, until it became an enormous shimmering bubble.

Suddenly, they were all inside – and in another place, hot and dry and sunny.

"It's Ancient Egypt!" gasped Jed.

The air was scented with spice and desert dust. Sand crunched under their feet as the cat led them onwards into a busy market full of people and animals.

Beyond were the banks of a vast river. The cat led them on to a sailing boat, filled with dates and fruit. The boat sailed upriver, passing between fields of grain. Jed and Ruby gazed around but nobody stopped or stared at them at all.

After a while, they reached a landing stage.

Jed and Ruby got off the boat and the cat

led them towards a waiting chariot. They

held on tightly as the driver flicked the reins.

Off raced the horses along the wide road.

The chariot stopped at the entrance of a grand palace.

"Meow!" called the cat, taking Ruby and Jed into a great hall, full of musicians and dancers. There, on a golden throne, sat a beautiful woman. She was smiling at them in a mysterious but friendly way.

"She's the only one who can see us," Jed said.

"The Princess!" gasped Ruby.

Then, in front of them, they saw a necklace. The wings were made from turquoise stones and the bird's body and head was gold. One gleaming stone was left, ready to set into place. This is why the cat had brought them here. The cat had chosen them to free the princess from a curse.

Ruby picked up the stone. The surface was carved with strange signs. As she placed the stone into Jed's palm, the gem glowed.

"It must be magical," Ruby said.

"It belongs in the necklace, doesn't it?"

Jed agreed. "I think the cat wants us to make the necklace complete." As they put the stone back, the cat began to purr loudly.

Suddenly they were outside, in the blazing sun of the courtyard. A blast of trumpets echoed around them. All the people lifted their heads – and became as still and silent as statues or paintings.

The cat gave a strange cry. Everything
shimmered and shone around them. The
next moment, the air smelt like home again
and they were back in their own time. The
cat was still with them, purring smugly.

Chapter 5
The Princess

"Ruby? Jed?" Mrs Brown was calling. "Are you okay? Your mum will be home in a moment." The cat had curled herself up behind the chair again.

"How," said Ruby, "can we get her back to the museum?"

"I don't know," said Jed, looking worried.

Mum had only been home a moment when the doorbell rang.

"Who can that be?" Mum opened the door. They all stared. Outside, in the dark, was a tall, elegant woman with large painted eyes. She was wrapped in an ancient shawl and her dark hair frizzed wildly around her head. She carried a large, battered straw basket under her arm.

"Good evening!" she began, in a voice that was as soft as a cat's purr.

"I'm Professor Akhten from the museum." Opening her basket, she held out two envelopes in her long, ring-encrusted fingers.

"Good news! Your children have won Young Egyptologist prizes."

The professor gave a dazzling smile. "Our records show your children often visit the museum." Mum nodded.

"Especially the Egyptian Galleries."

Jed and Ruby nodded.

"We...we were there today," they stammered. Could this mysterious professor be who they thought she was? She had not stepped into the light.

The professor smiled.

"Yes, it was a day when we needed
observant children about."

Ruby and Jed opened the envelopes.

"Sleepover tickets!" they cried.

"There's one for you as well." The professor
gave Mum a ticket too.

Mum went pink with excitement.

"Oh, please do come in," she said. "I'll just
pop into the kitchen and put the kettle on."

The professor stayed in the shadows outside.
"I'm sorry. I can't come in," she explained,
"I have an important job to do."
She gave a curious low whistle.
"Meow!" Out from Jed's room ran the cat.
She twirled and whirled round the professor's
ankles then leaped into the open basket,
purring happily.

"Sorry. It's later than I thought, I must go!" said the professor. Clutching the basket to her chest, the professor winked. "Well done, you two," she whispered. "The Egyptian cat is safe again. By placing the gem in the necklace you broke the curse that kept me as a ghost." Then she hurried off into the night.

"What a strange woman," Mum said.

"And what a wonderful Princess," Jed whispered to Ruby.

Next morning, Mum checked that the sleepover tickets really were okay. Just as she was logging off from the museum website, she stopped.

"Look at this!" There, on Mum's tablet, was the image of an ancient Egyptian Princess. "It says here that she's supposed to haunt the museum. You know, she reminds me of somebody, but I can't think who."

Jed and Ruby just smiled.

the Museum

First published in 2014 by
Franklin Watts
338 Euston Road
London
NW1 3BH

Franklin Watts Australia
Level 17/207 Kent Street
Sydney
NSW 2000

Text © Penny Dolan 2014
Illustration © Andy Elkerton 2014

The rights of Penny Dolan to be identified as
the author and Andy Elkerton as the
illustrator of this Work have been asserted in
accordance with the Copyright, Designs and
Patents Act, 1988.

Series Editor: Melanie Palmer
Series Advisor: Catherine Glavina
Series Designer: Cathryn Gilbert

A CIP catalogue record for this book is
available from the British Library.

ISBN 978 1 4451 3345 4 (hbk)
ISBN 978 1 4451 3346 1 (pbk)
ISBN 978 1 4451 3347 8 (ebook)
ISBN 978 1 4451 3348 5 (library ebook)

Printed in China

Franklin Watts is a division of Hachette
Children's Books, an Hachette UK company.
www.hachette.co.uk